A WORDLESS GRAPHIC NOVEL

LOONEY TUNES™

HIGH-RISE HIJINKS

by Ivan Cohen
illustrated by Scott Gross

PICTURE WINDOW BOOKS
a capstone imprint

Published by Picture Window Books,
an imprint of Capstone
1710 Roe Crest Drive
North Mankato, Minnesota 56003
capstonepub.com

Library of Congress Cataloging-in-Publication Data
Names: Cohen, Ivan, author. | Gross, Scott, illustrator.
Title: High-rise hijinks / by Ivan Cohen ; illustrated by Scott Gross.
Other titles: Looney Tunes.
Description: North Mankato, Minnesota : Picture Window Books, an
    imprint of Capstone, [2021] | Series: Looney Tunes wordless graphic
    novels | Audience: Ages 5–7. | Audience: Grades K–2. | Summary:
    "When Tweety moves into Sylvester's apartment building, the
    poor puddy tat finds himself put out. Can Sylvester slip past
    Tweety's defenses to return to his home-sweet-home?"—Provided
    by publisher.
Identifiers: LCCN 2021002473 (print) | LCCN 2021002474 (ebook)
    | ISBN 9781663910141 (hardcover) | ISBN 9781663920348
    (paperback) | ISBN 9781663910110 (ebook pdf)
Subjects: LCSH: Graphic novels. | CYAC: Graphic novels. | Stories
    without words. | Tweety Pie (Fictitious character)—Fiction. |
    Sylvester (Fictitious character)—Fiction. | Apartment houses—
    Fiction.
Classification: LCC PZ7.7.C64 Hi 2021 (print) | LCC PZ7.7.C64 (ebook)
    | DDC 741.5/973—dc23
LC record available at https://lccn.loc.gov/2021002473
LC ebook record available at https://lccn.loc.gov/2021002474

Designed by Dina Her

Printed in the United States   4620

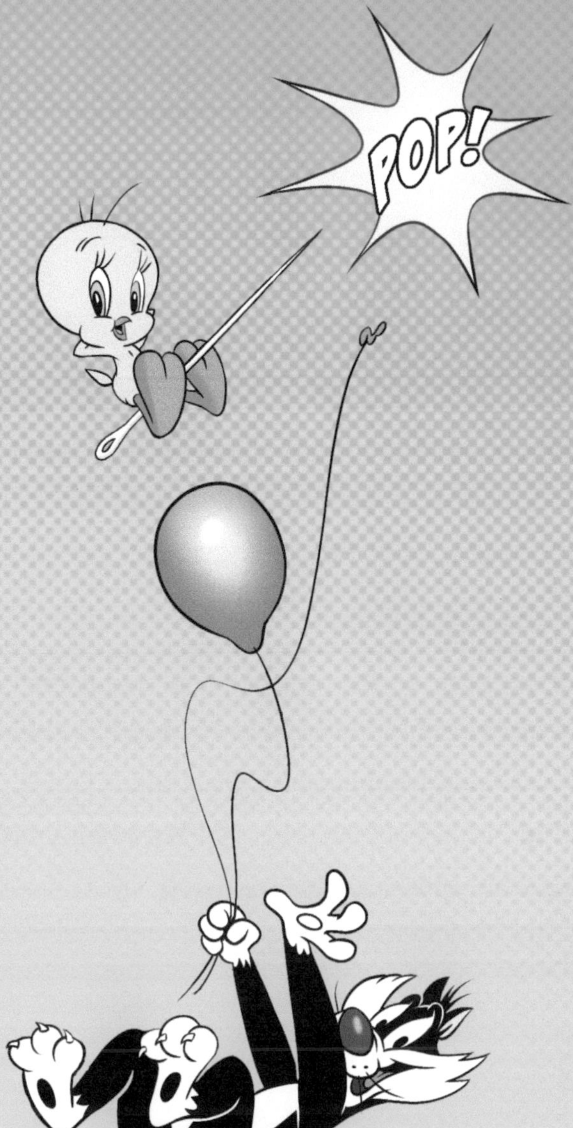
POP!

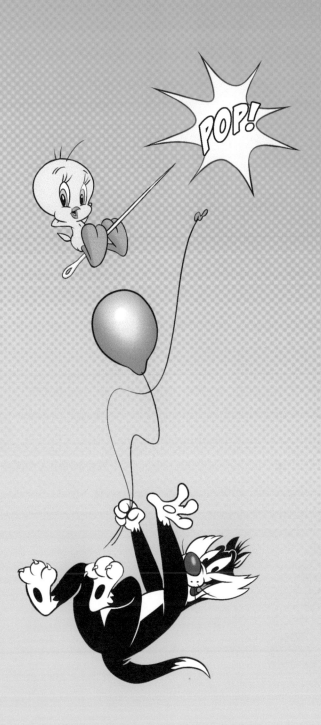

Meet

TWEETY AND SYLVESTER

Tweety

Tweety is always on the lookout for a "puddy tat" who wants to cause him trouble. The small, yellow bird knows that bigger animals think they can get the upper hand—or paw—over him. But when a cat like Sylvester sneaks up on him, Tweety knows how to take care of himself.

Sylvester

Sylvester is a black-and-white "tuxedo" cat who fancies fresh food. Although he always tries his best, his plans usually fall flat. But Sylvester isn't one to just give up. After muttering "sufferin' succotash" under his breath, he simply dreams up a new scheme to get what he wants.

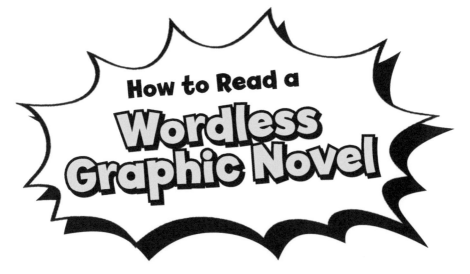

How to Read a Wordless Graphic Novel

Wordless graphic novels are easy to read. Boxes called panels show you how to follow the story. Look at the panels from left to right and top to bottom. Read any sound effects as you go.

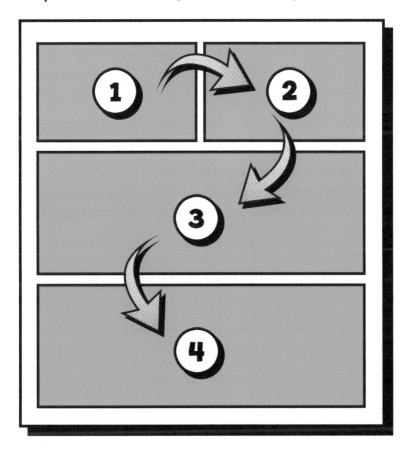

By putting the panels together, you'll understand the whole story!

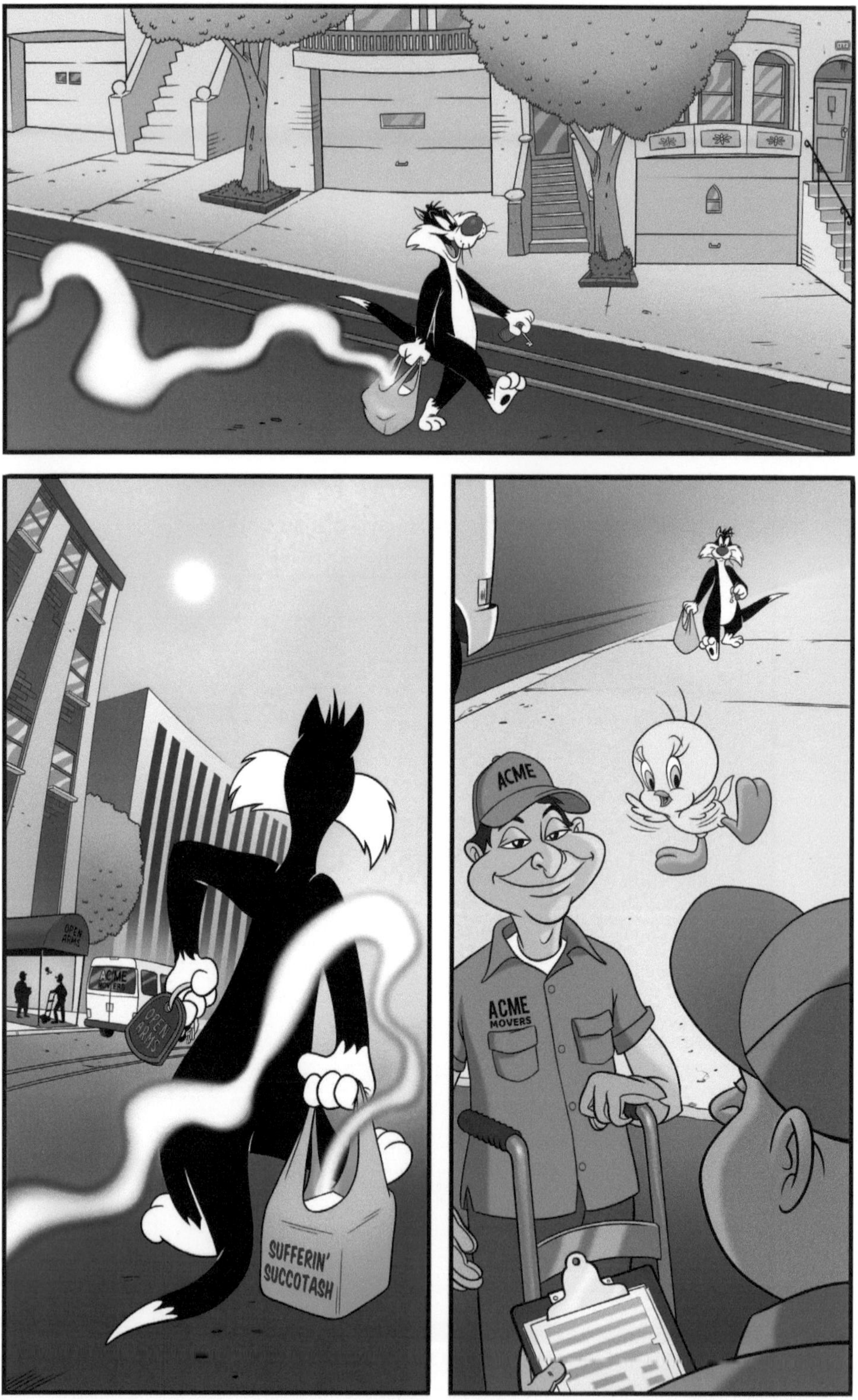
OPEN ARMS
ACME MOVERS
OPEN ARMS
SUFFERIN' SUCCOTASH
ACME
ACME MOVERS

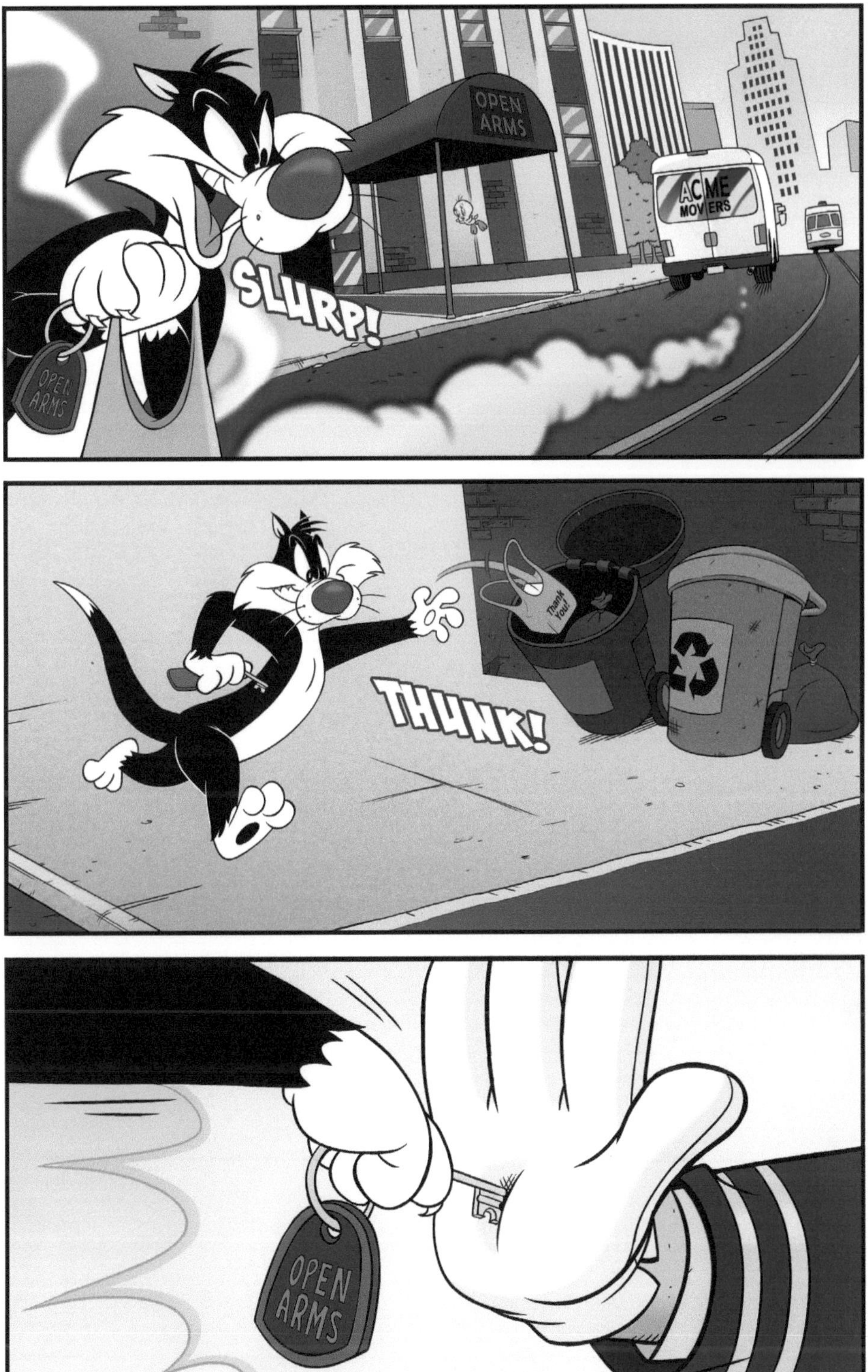
OPEN ARMS
ACME MOVERS
OPEN ARMS
SLURP!
Thank You!
THUNK!
OPEN ARMS

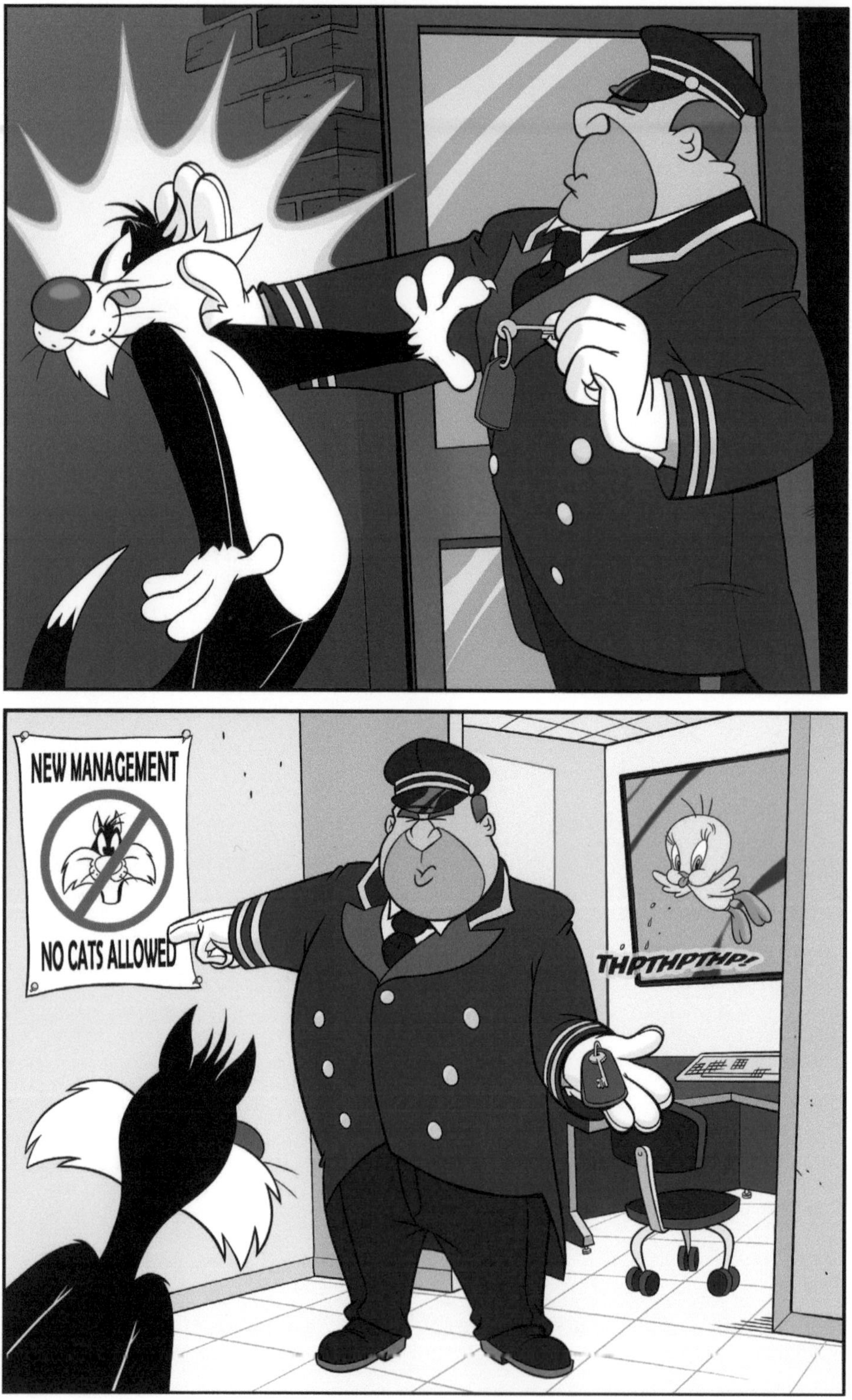
NEW MANAGEMENT
NO CATS ALLOWED
THPTHPTHP!

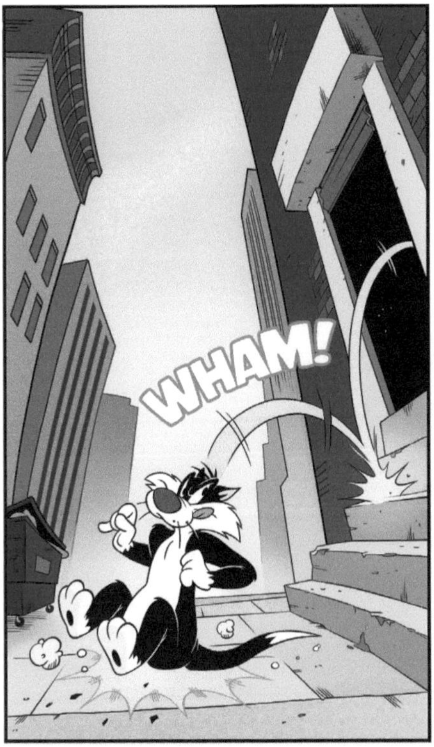
WHAM!

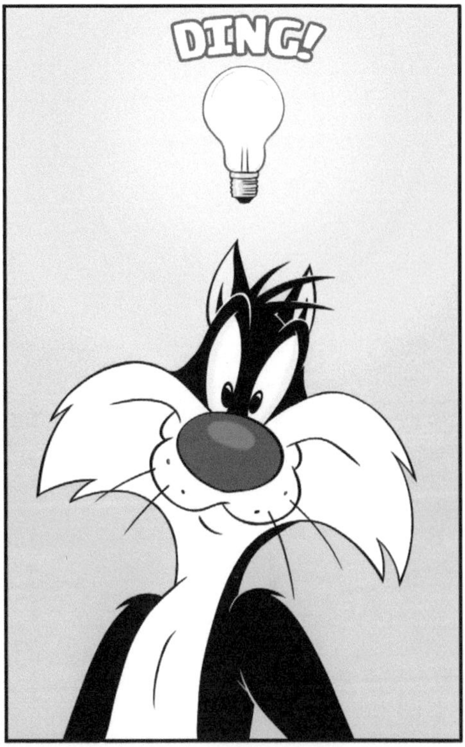
DING!

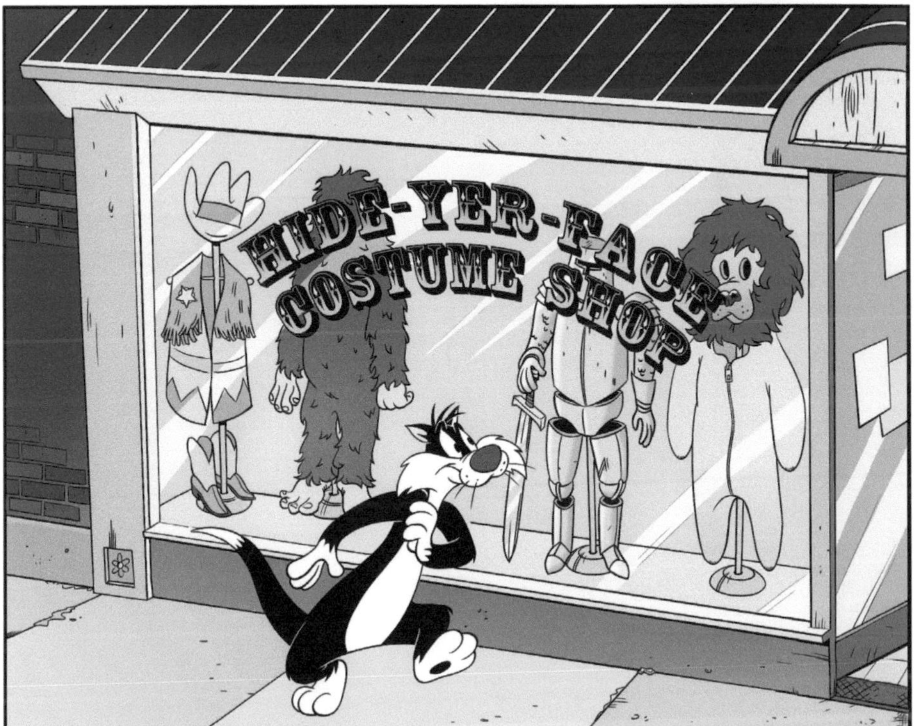
HIDE-YER-FACE
COSTUME SHOP

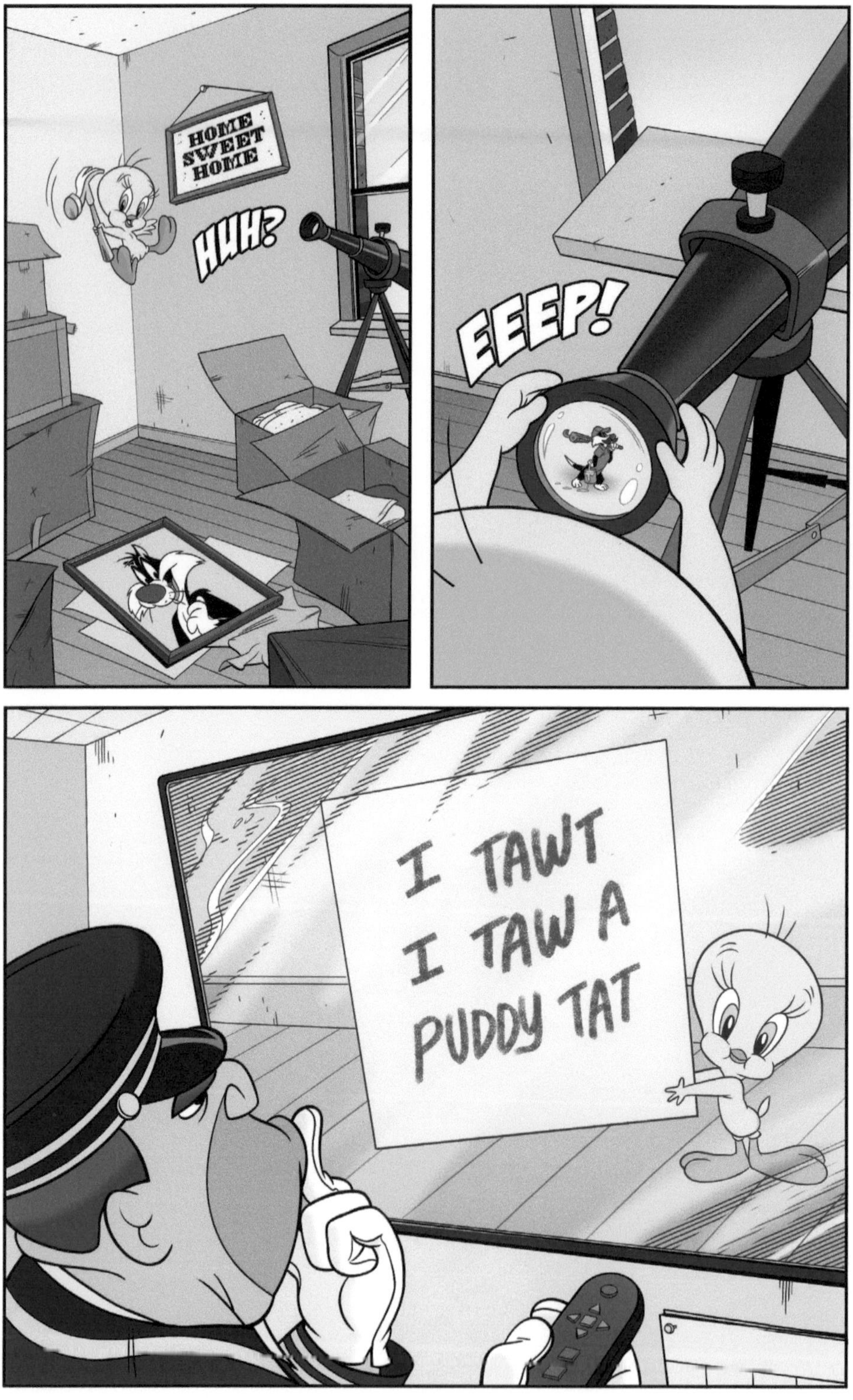
HOME SWEET HOME
HUH?
EEEP!
I TAWT I TAW A PUDDY TAT

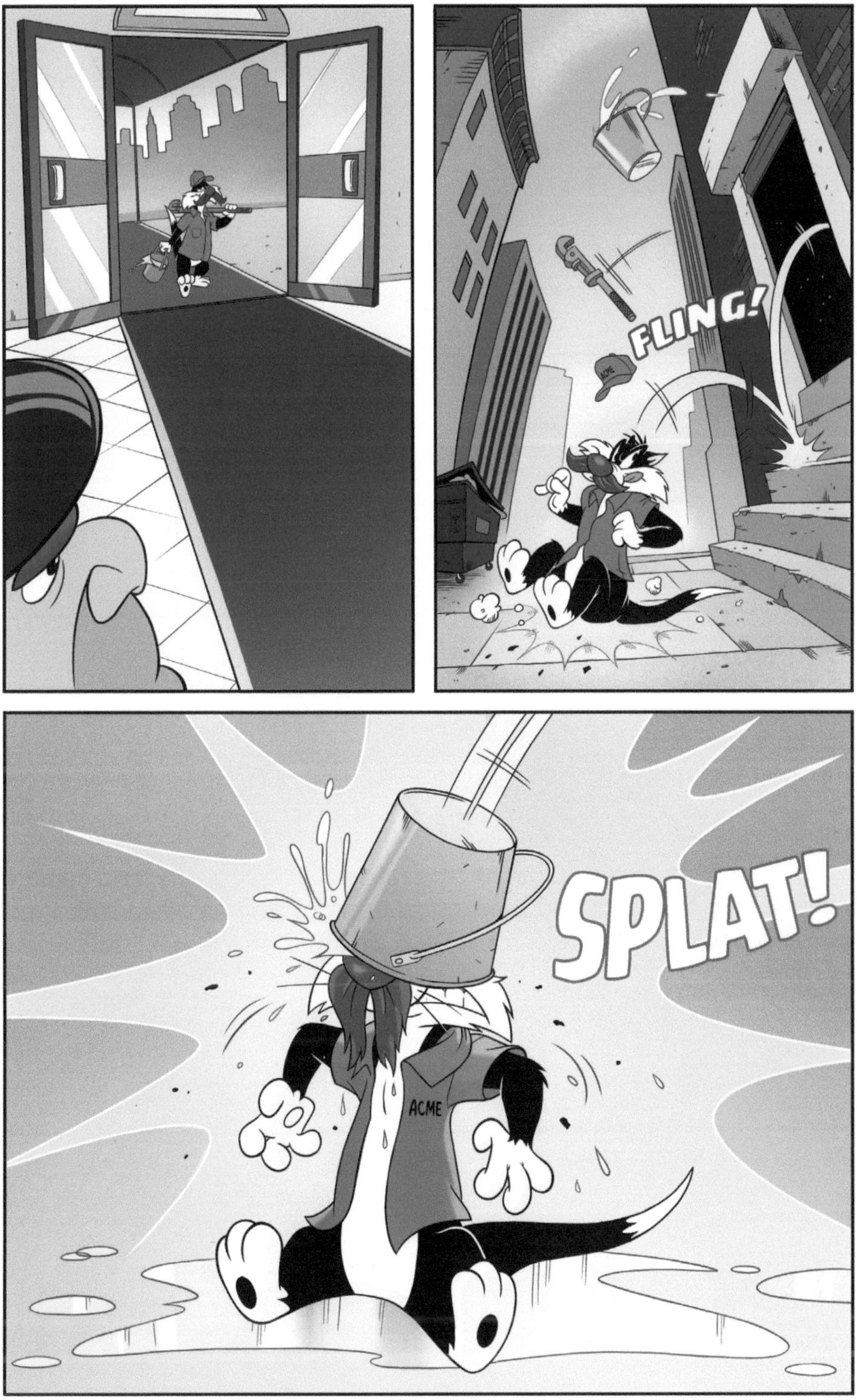
FLING!
ACME
ACME
SPLAT!
ACME

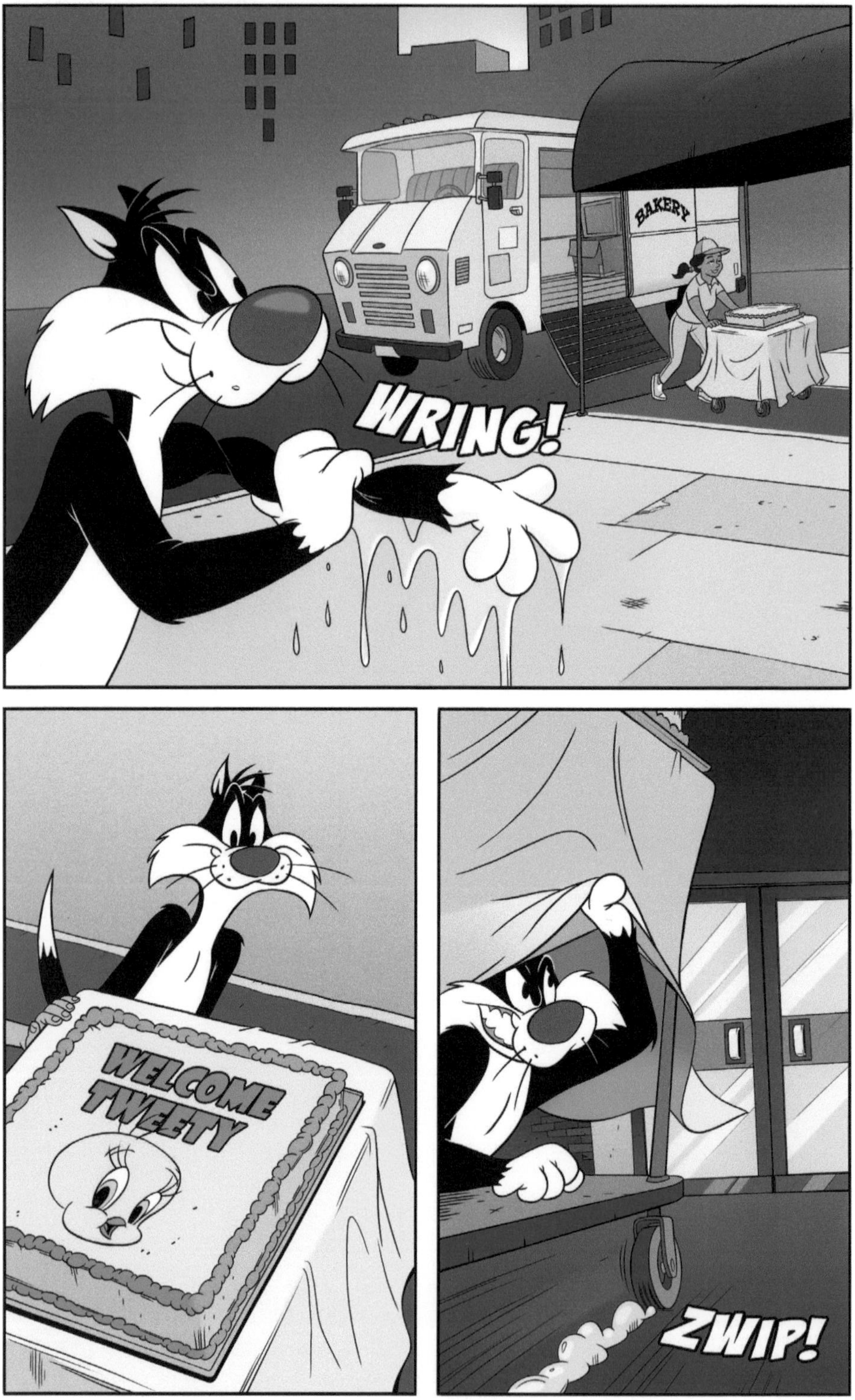
BAKERY
WRING!
WELCOME TWEETY
ZWIP!

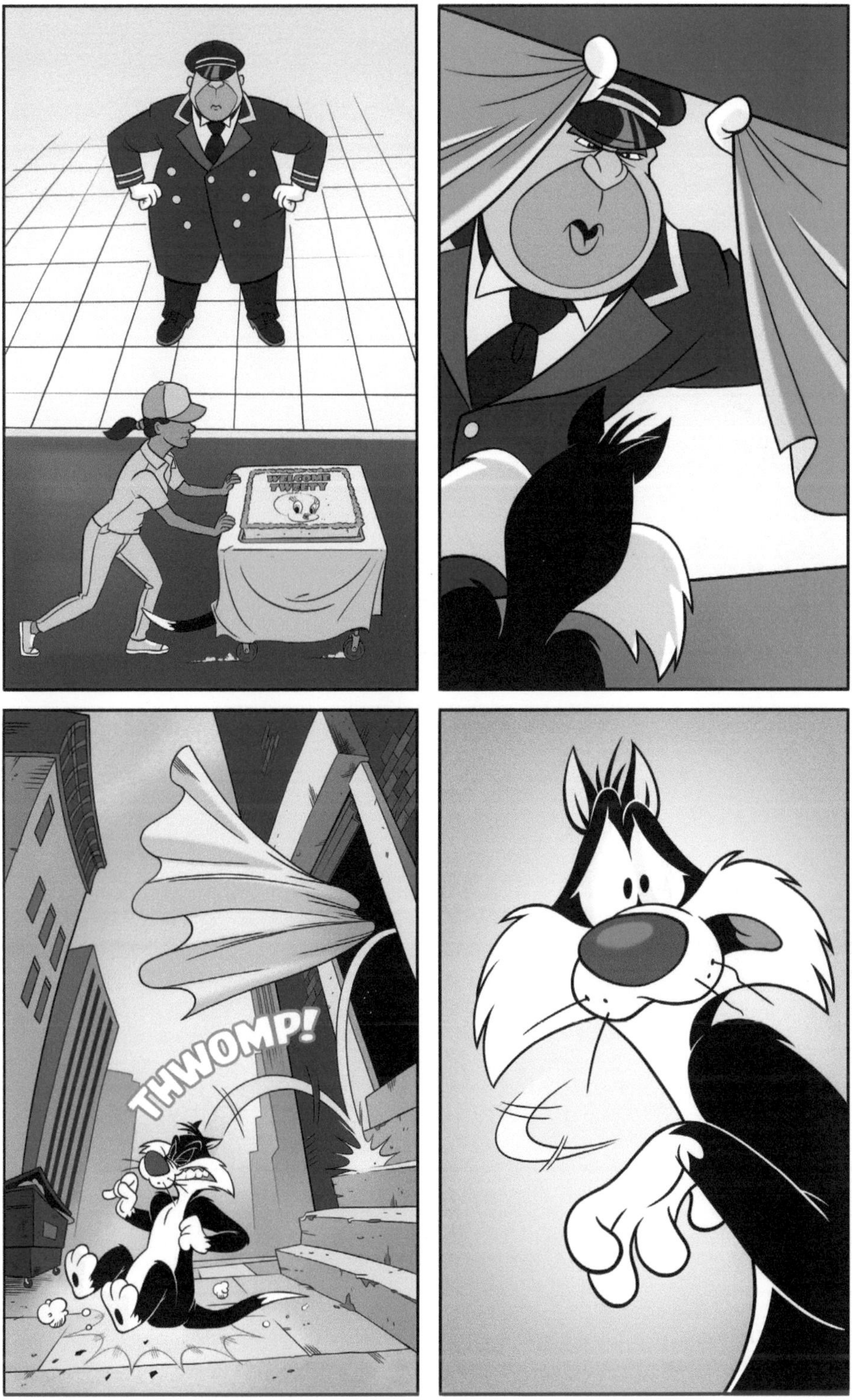
WELCOME TWEETY
THWOMP!

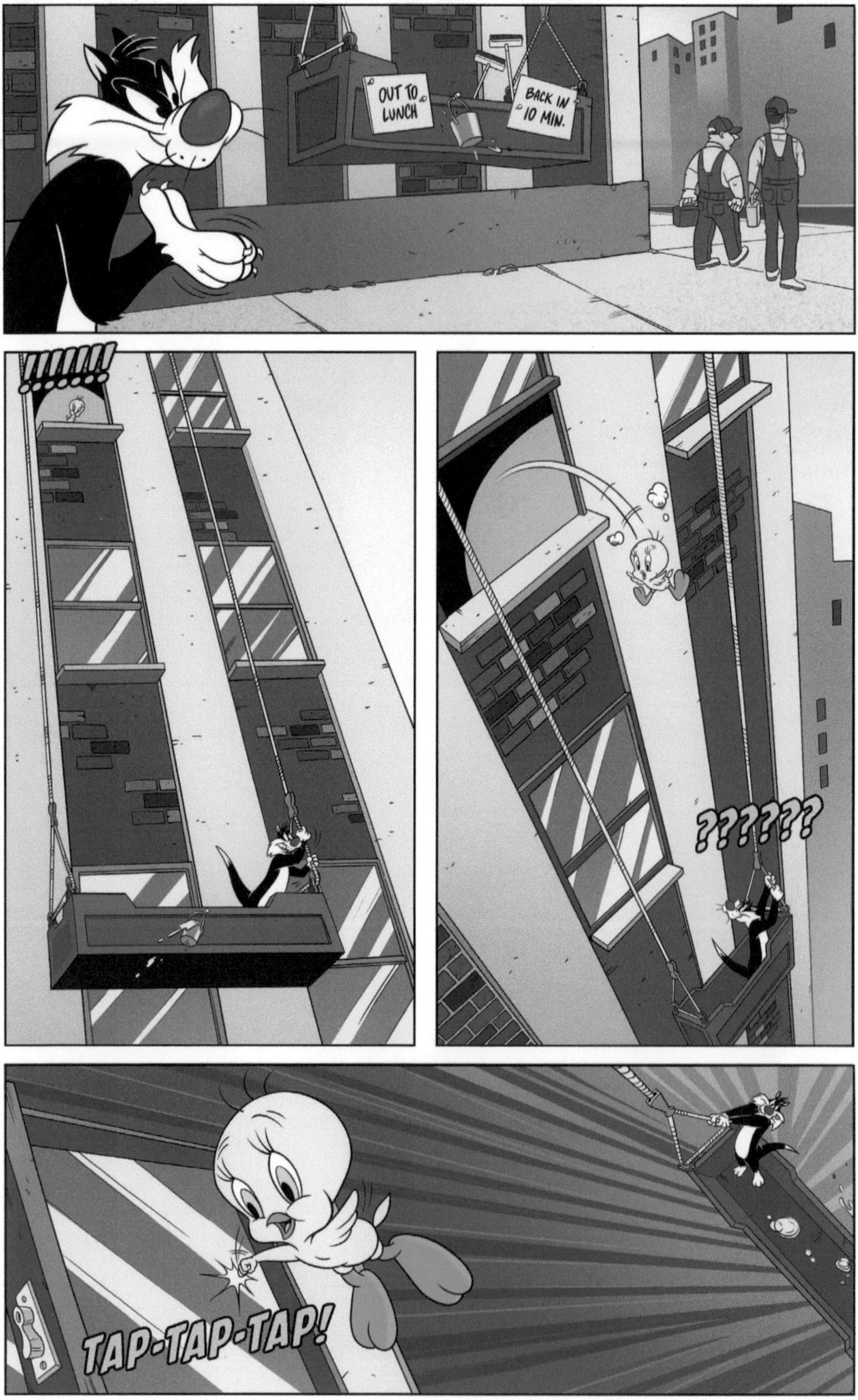
OUT TO LUNCH
BACK IN 10 MIN.
!!!!!!!
??????
TAP-TAP-TAP!

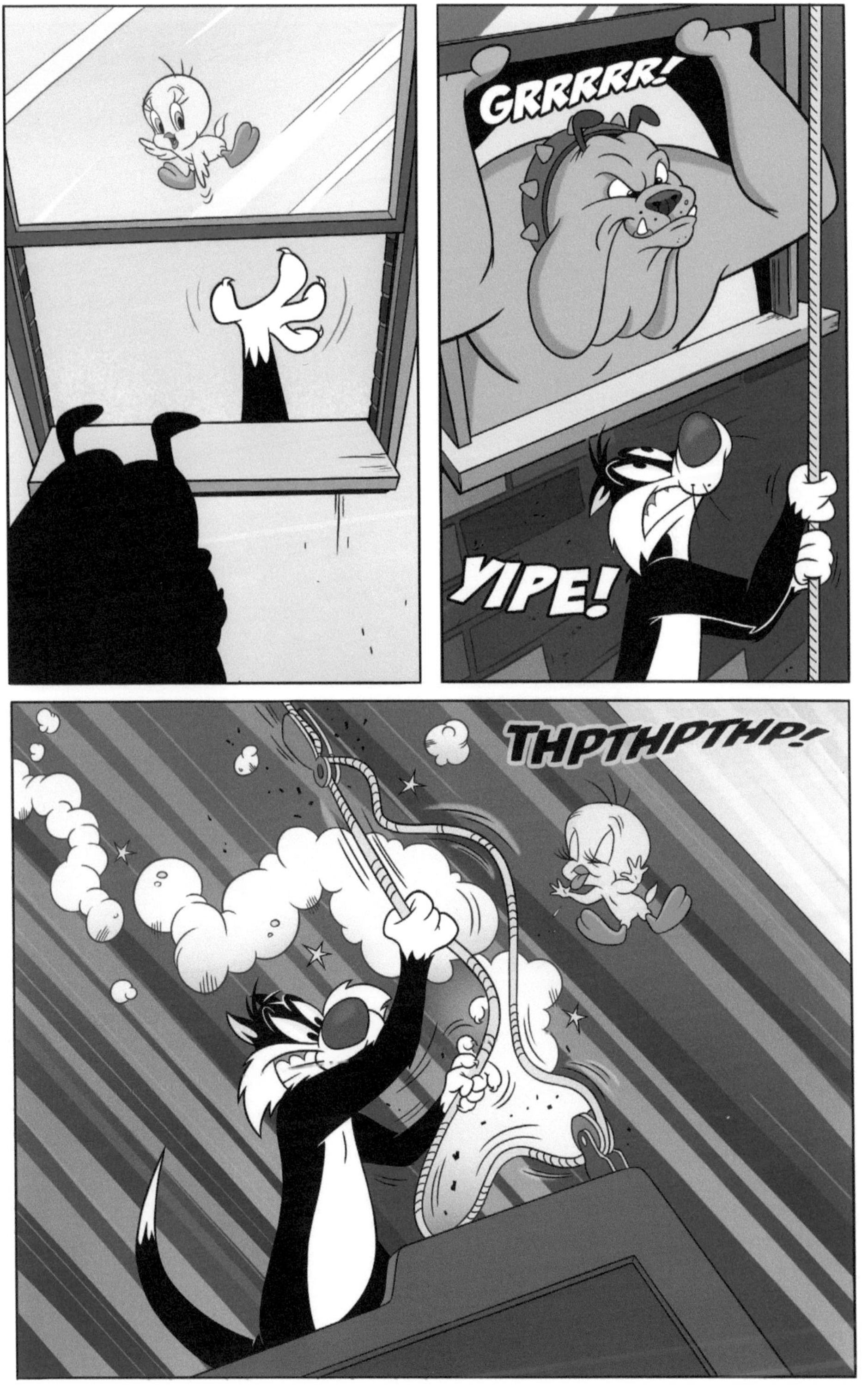
GRRRRR!
YIPE!
THPTHPTHP!

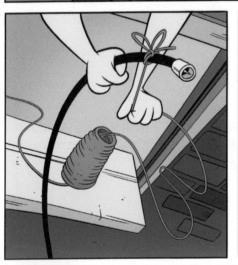

TOODLE-OO!

ZZZZT!

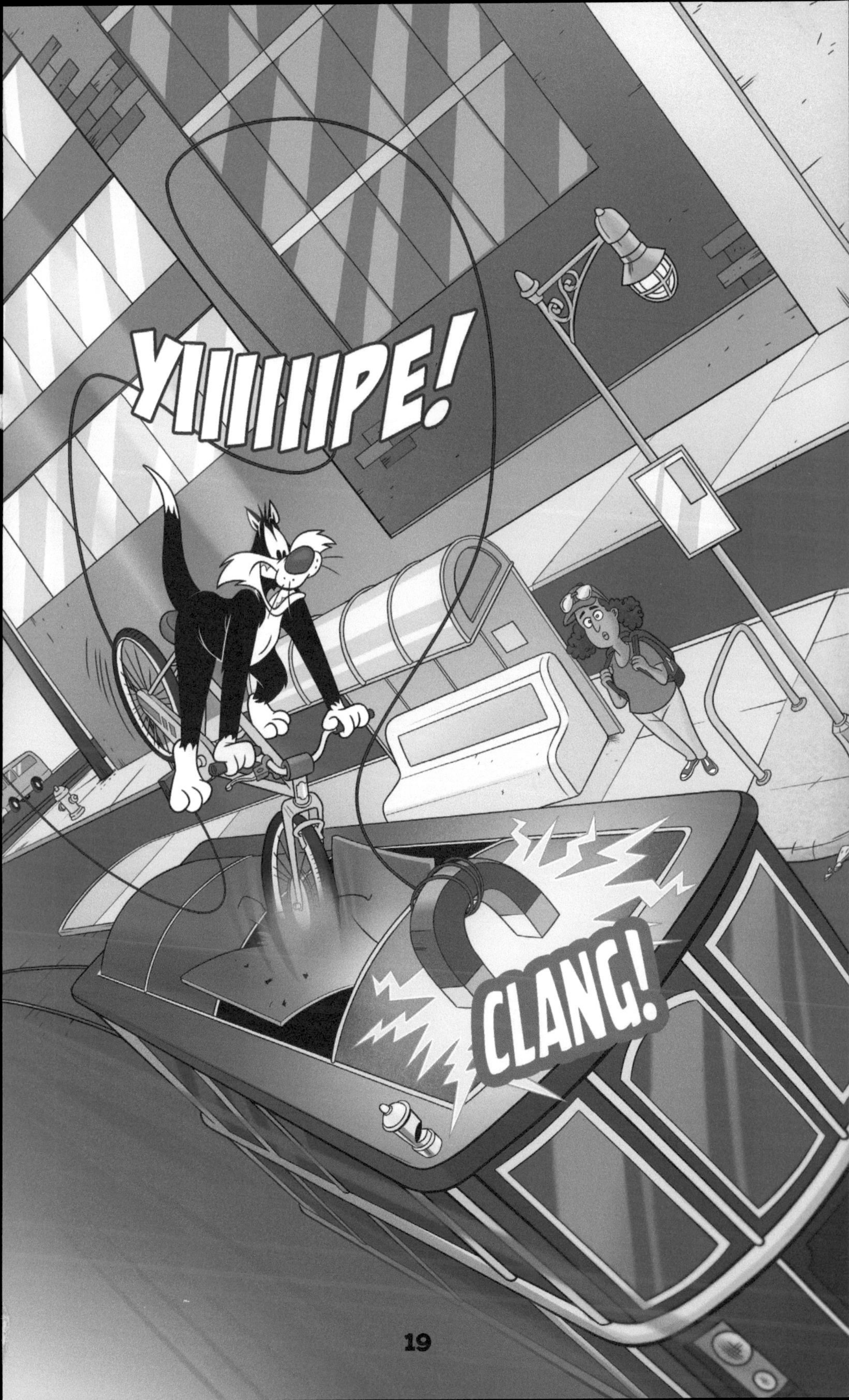
YIIIIIIPE!
CLANG!

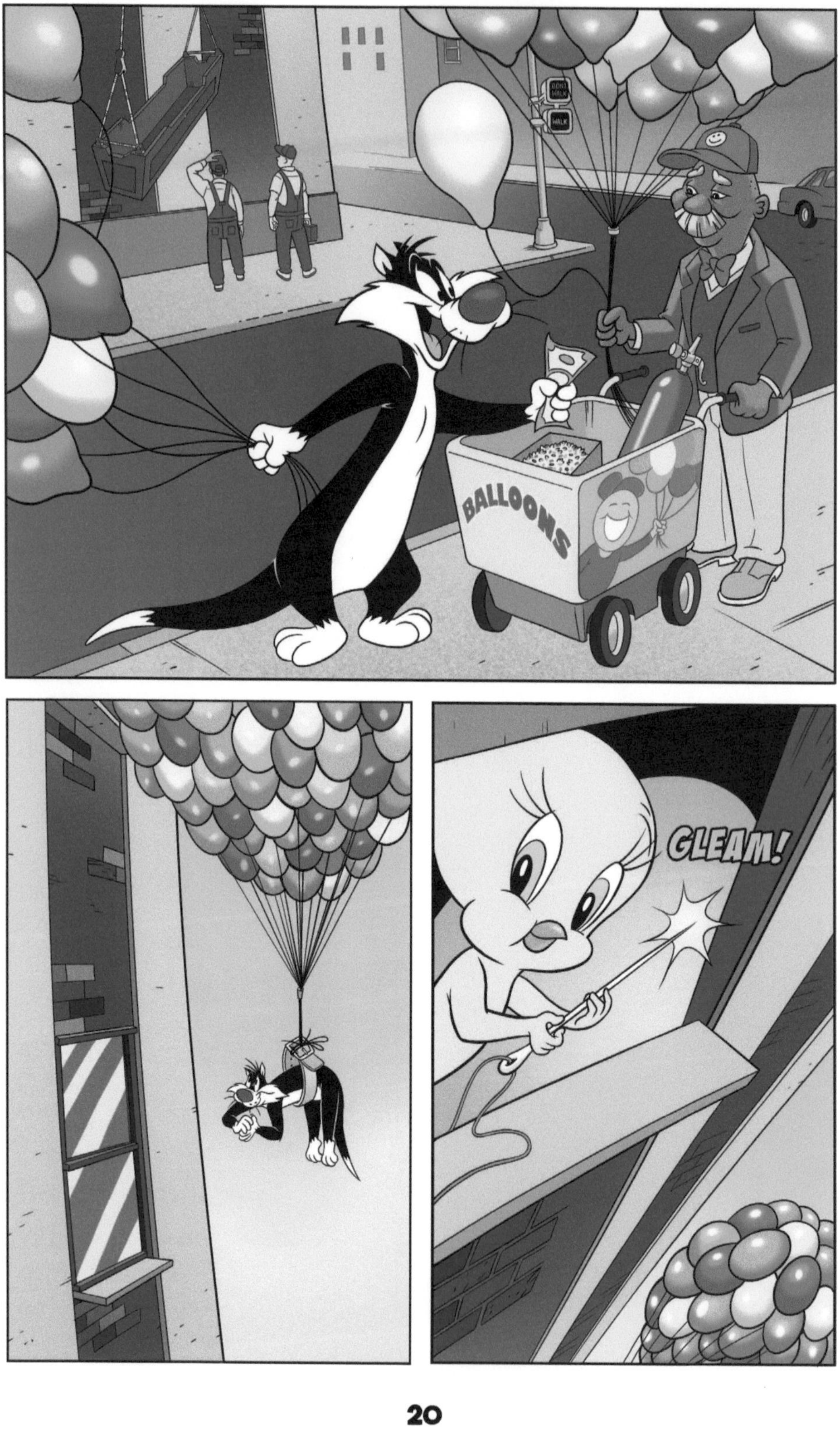
DON'T WALK
WALK
BALLOONS
GLEAM!

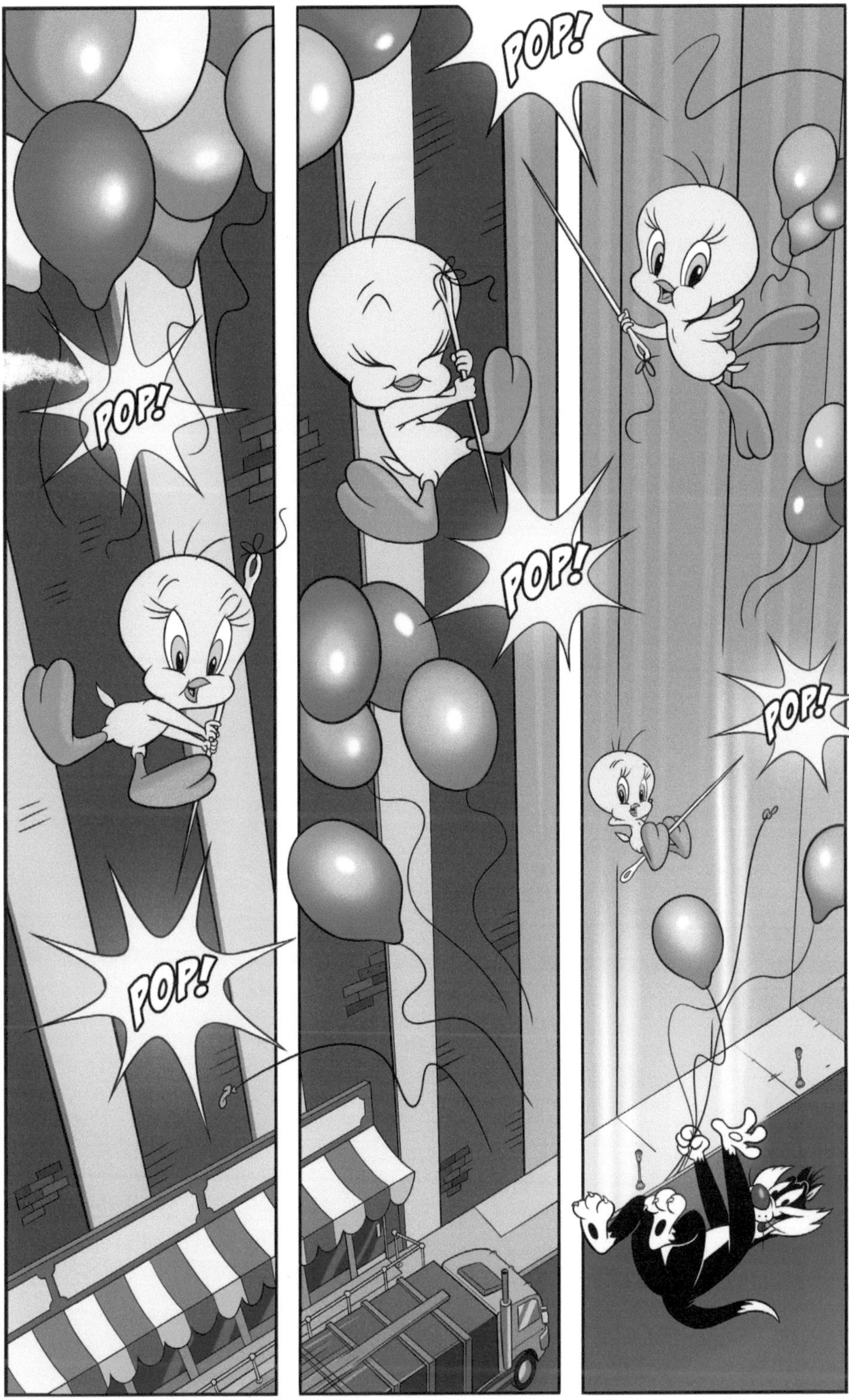
POP!
POP!
POP!
POP!
POP!
POP!

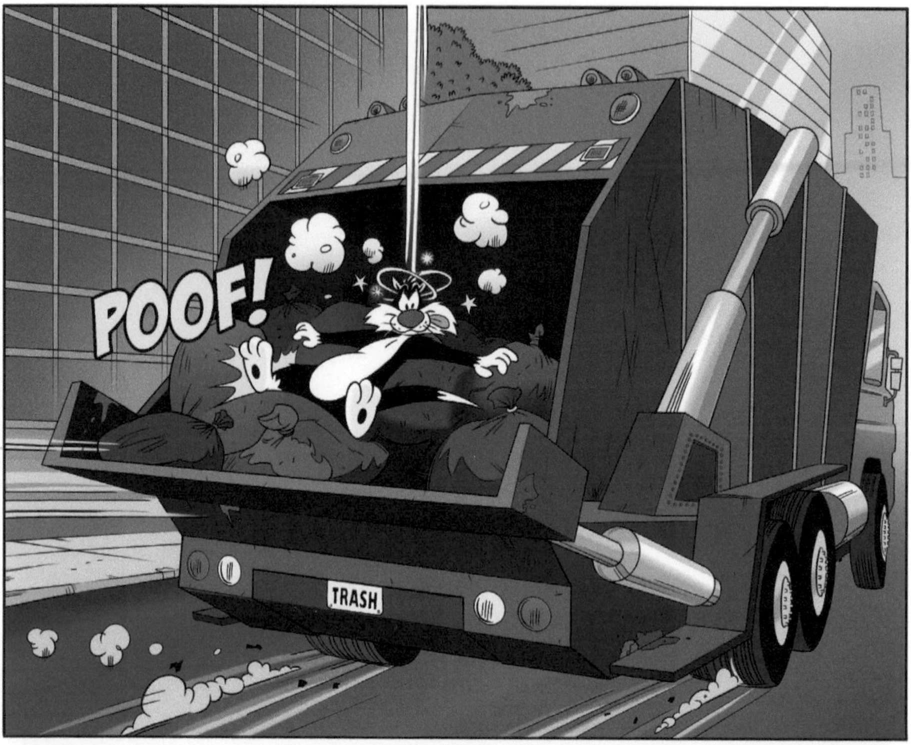
POOF!
TRASH

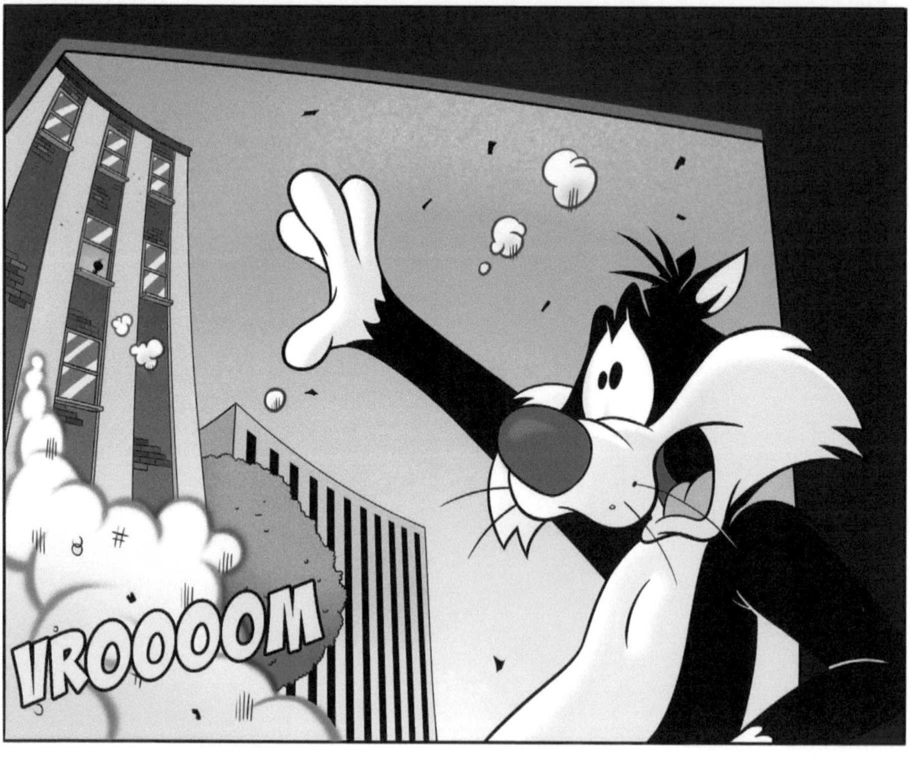
VROOOOM

HOME SWEET HOME
DRIZZLE DRIZZLE
NUH-UH

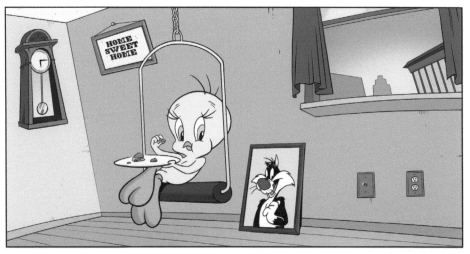

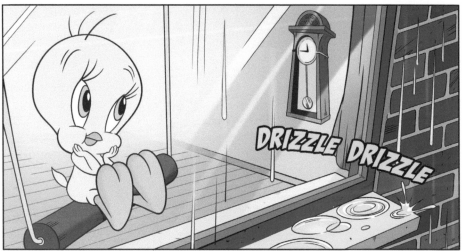

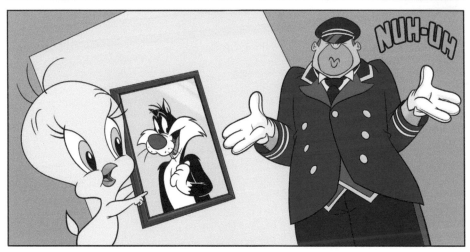

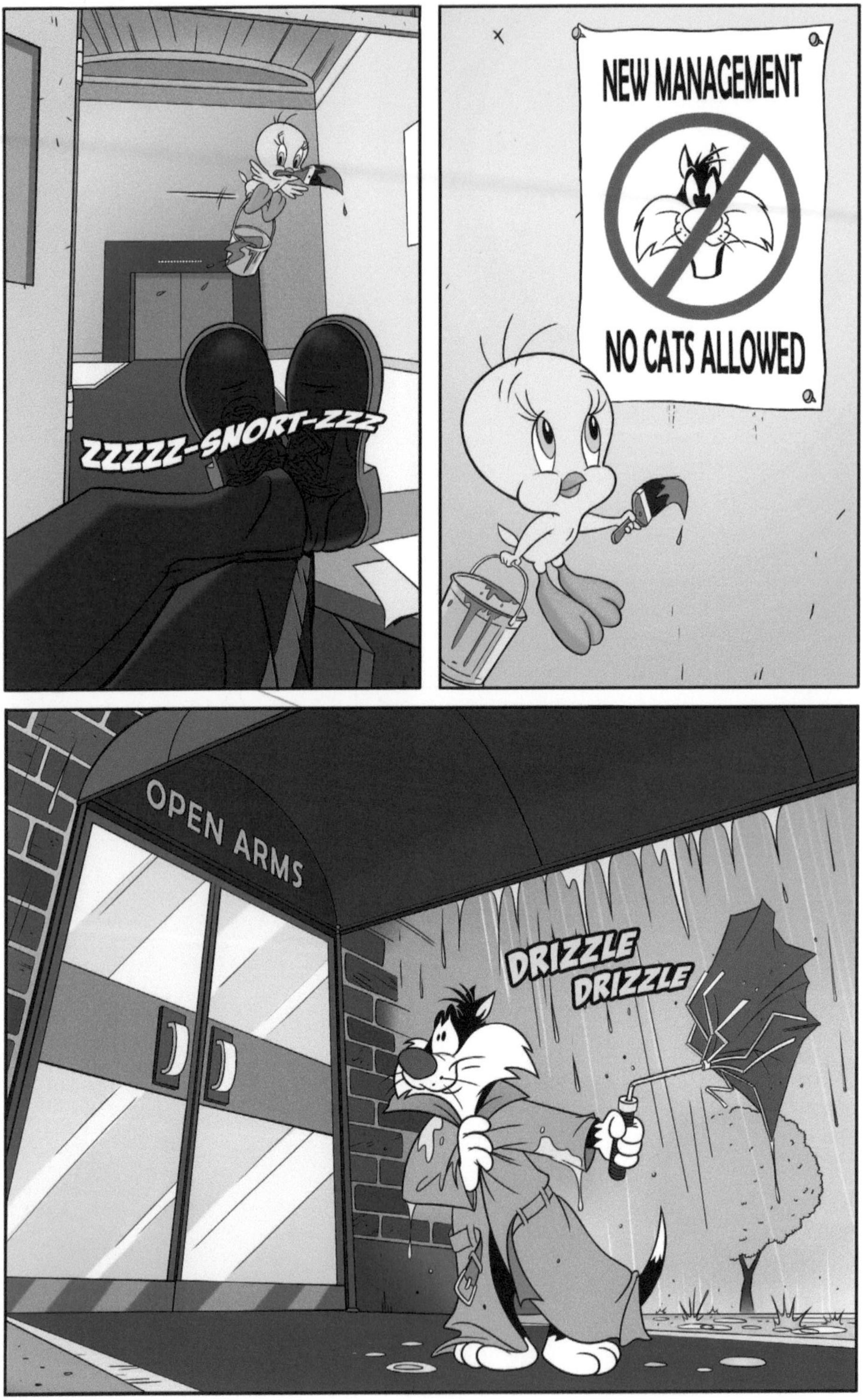
ZZZZZ-SNORT-ZZZ
NEW MANAGEMENT
NO CATS ALLOWED
OPEN ARMS
DRIZZLE
DRIZZLE

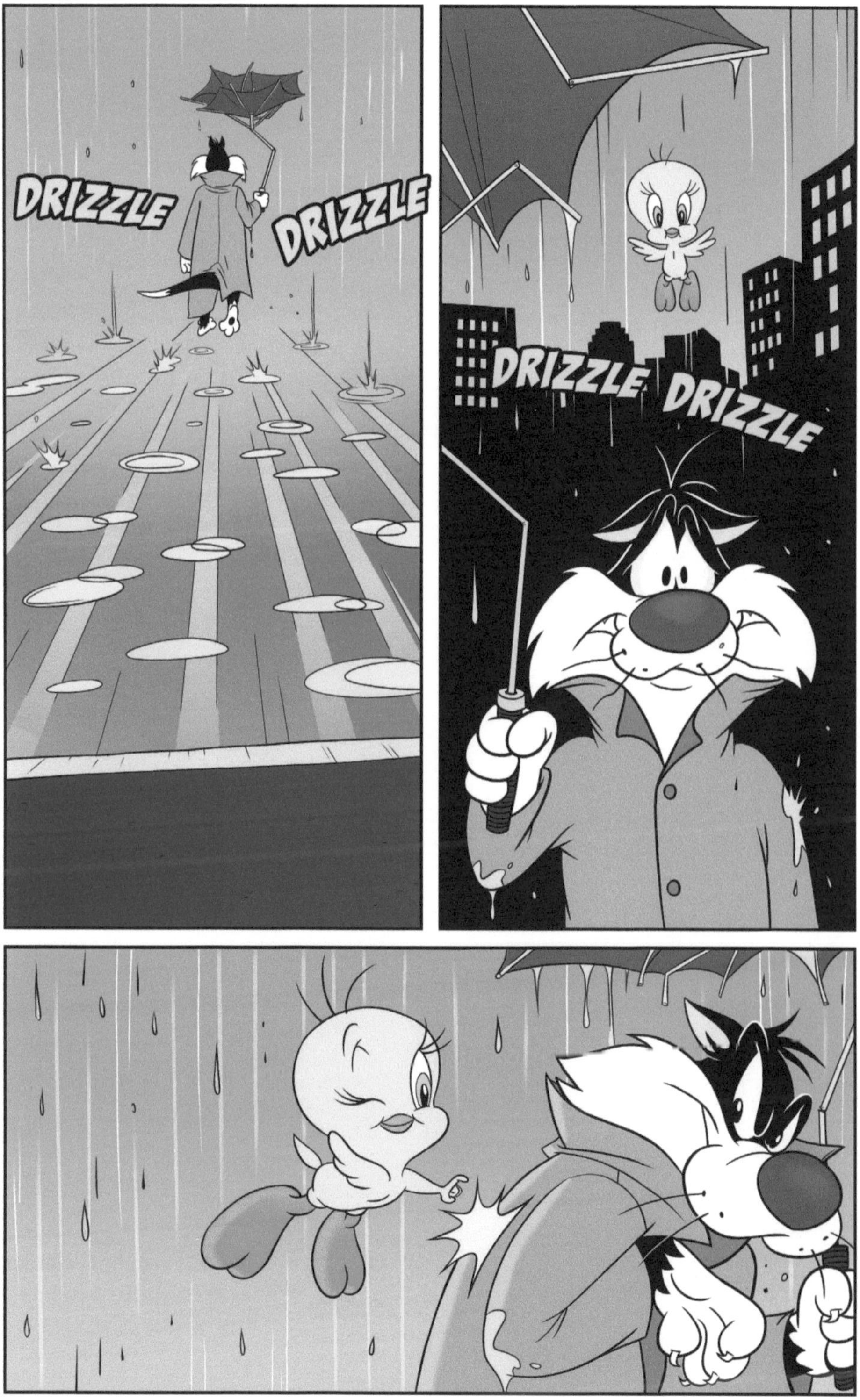
DRIZZLE
DRIZZLE
DRIZZLE
DRIZZLE

Panel Talk

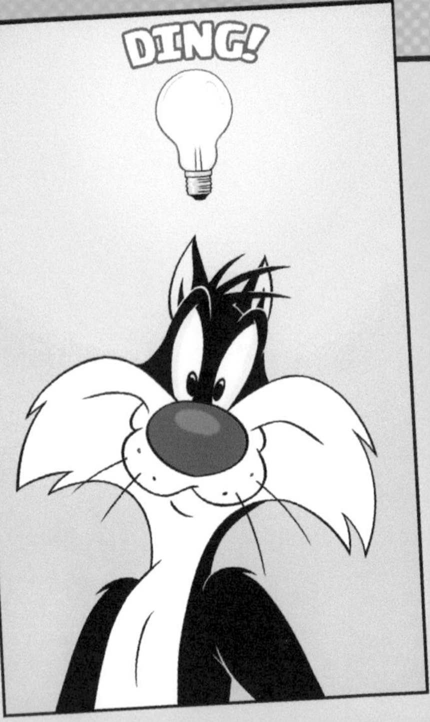
DING!

1. Why does Sylvester have a lightbulb above his head? What does it tell you about him?

2. What is Sylvester thinking in this panel? How do you know?

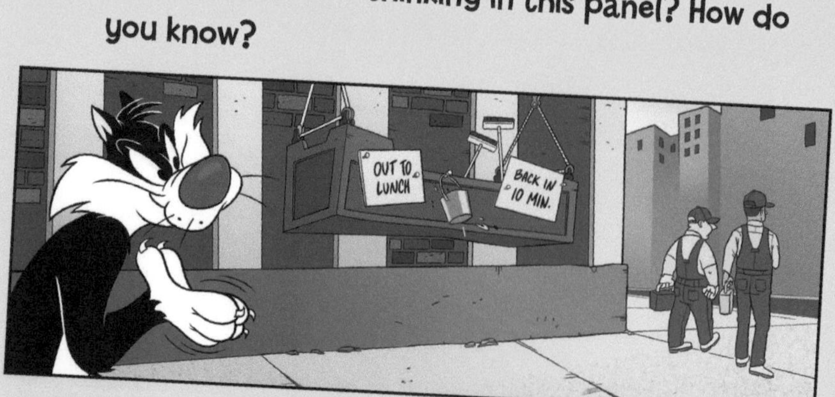
OUT TO LUNCH
BACK IN 10 MIN.

3. Why is Tweety holding Sylvester's picture? What is he asking the doorman?

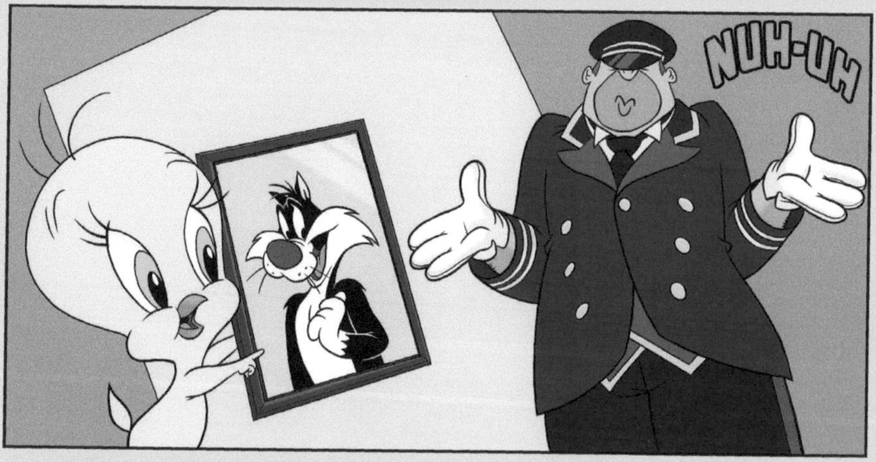
NUH-UH

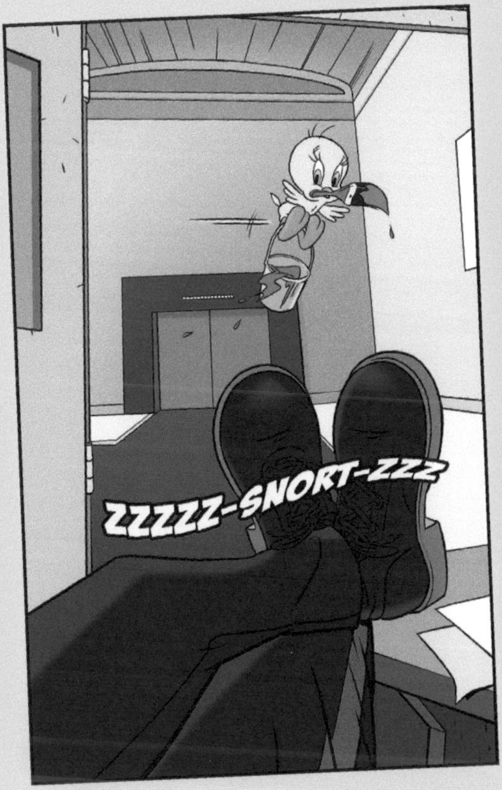
ZZZZZ-SNORT-ZZZ

4. What is the doorman doing in this panel? What clues tell you that?

LOONEY TUNES ™

Through the Years

Looney Tunes has entertained fans both young and old for more than 90 years. It all started back in 1930 with animated short films that ran in movie theaters. By 1970, these shorts leaped from big movie screens to small TV screens. From that point forward, generations of young fans have grown up watching these classic cartoons in their own homes.

What makes Looney Tunes so successful? Its amazing cast of characters, of course! Stars include Bugs Bunny, Porky Pig, Daffy Duck, Tweety, Sylvester, Marvin the Martian, Road Runner, and Wile E. Coyote. And don't forget their outrageous costars! Elmer Fudd, Yosemite Sam, Foghorn Leghorn, Pepé Le Pew, and the Tasmanian Devil add hilarious hijinks to every story.

With such a zany cast, it's no wonder Looney Tunes' return to the big screen often bursts beyond straight animation. Modern films have featured Bugs Bunny and his friends mixing things up with live-action sports and movie stars in *Space Jam* and *Looney Tunes: Back in Action*. And in 2021, the film *Space Jam: A New Legacy* has them destined for even more out-of-this-world adventures!

About the Author

Ivan Cohen has written comics, children's books, and TV shows featuring some of the world's most popular characters, including Teen Titans Go!, Batman, Spider-Man, Wonder Woman, Superman, the Justice League, and the Avengers. Ivan looks forward to reading this book with his wife and son in their home in New York City.

About the Illustrator

When **Scott Gross** watched his first Looney Tunes cartoons as a child, they were already classics. He knew he was seeing something of quality from an earlier era that had stood the test of time and was still funny. Since then he's become the author and illustrator of many stories starring Bugs Bunny and the gang. In each one he strives to preserve the timeless characters and humor we have all grown to love.